# The Intimacy of Love —

## A Companion Workbook
## for Married Couples

By Pastor Candy LaFlora

*The Intimacy of Love –*
*A Companion Workbook for Married Couples*
ISBN: 979-8-9900524-6-8
Copyright © 2025 by Candy LaFlora
Step N Wool Publishing Inc.
P. O. Box 205 Olympia Fields, IL 60461
www.stepwool.com

Cover Design: Candy LaFlora
Text Design: Lisa Simpson
www.simpsonproductions.net

# Contents

*"True love doesn't fade with time—it grows deeper with every trial, every triumph, and every tear. When rooted in God, love becomes eternal—an unbreakable bond that outlives even the passing of years."*

*— Candy LaFlora*

# 1

# Created for Intimacy

**Scripture Focus: Genesis 2:18, 24**

Prayer: "Father, thank You for creating us for relationship. Help us to grow in oneness and walk in the unity of love You intended."

**Reflect & Connect:**

- What does "becoming one" mean to you personally?

- In what ways do you feel most connected with your spouse?

**Today's Assignment:**

Write a love letter to your spouse telling them one thing you appreciate about how they love you.

**Group Discussion Application:**

- What does true intimacy look like to you beyond physical closeness?

- How do you keep intimacy alive when life feels busy or stressful?

*"Love endures long
and is patient and kind;
love never is envious nor boils
over with jealousy, is not boastful
or vainglorious, does not
display itself haughtily.*

**1 Corinthians 13:4**

# 2

# Love Is the Foundation

**Scripture Focus: 1 Corinthians 13:4–8**

Prayer: "Lord, teach us to love with patience, kindness, and grace."

**Reflect & Connect:**

- Which part of this love chapter do you struggle with most?

- Share a time your spouse loved you in a 1 Corinthians 13 way.

**Today's Assignment:**

Memorize one verse from this chapter together and recite it to each other before bed for one week.

**Group Discussion Application:**

- How do you practice love when you don't feel like it?

- What's a creative way you've shown love that surprised your spouse?

"*Intimacy is more than a physical connection—it's about being fully known and still fully loved. It's about building a bond so strong that life's storms can't break it and daily routine can't dull it.*"

# 3

# When Seasons Shift

**Scripture Focus: Ecclesiastes 3:1–8**

Prayer: "God, help us recognize the season we are in and respond to it with love and faith."

**Reflect & Connect:**

- What season is your marriage currently in?

- How can you support each other more in this season?

**Assignment:**

Create a "season survival kit": List 3 ways to protect your connection during difficult seasons.

**Group Discussion Application:**

- How do you handle changes or challenges as a team?

- What helped you thrive in a difficult season of your marriage?

Trying to mold your spouse into your
image creates frustration
and resistance.

# 4

# Communication & Grace

**Scripture Focus: James 1:19, Ephesians 4:29**

Prayer: "Help us to listen, speak truth in love, and build each other up."

**Reflect & Connect:**

- What are your biggest communication strengths? Weaknesses?

- How do you prefer to be approached during conflict?

**Assignment:**

Do a "No Complaining" challenge for 24 hours. Instead, speak one encouraging word every hour.

**Group Discussion Application:**

- What's one communication tool that has helped your marriage?

- How do you show grace when your spouse says something that hurts?

*It is not conceited (arrogant and inflated with pride); it is not rude (unmannerly) and does not act unbecomingly. Love (God's love in us) does not insist on its own rights or its own way, for it is not self-seeking; it is not touchy or fretful or resentful; it takes no account of the evil done to it [it pays no attention to a suffered wrong].*

1 Corinthians 13:5

# 5

## Forgiveness & Restoration

**Scripture Focus: Colossians 3:13, Matthew 18:21–22**

Prayer: "Jesus, give us hearts that forgive quickly and love deeply."

**Reflect & Connect:**

- Share a time you had to forgive. How did it restore love?

- Why is forgiveness a gift you give to yourself too?

**Assignment:**

Write something you're releasing, then pray together and tear it up.

**Group Discussion Application:**

- What makes forgiveness difficult, and how do you overcome that?

- How do you rebuild trust after a conflict?

Somewhere along the way, between the bills, the responsibilities, the kids, the calendar, and the never-ending "to-do" list, many couples lose their sense of play.

# 6

# Rekindling Romance

**Scripture Focus: Song of Solomon 1:2–4**

Prayer: "Lord, ignite passion and affection between us again."

**Reflect & Connect:**

- What small things make you feel desired?
- What's your spouse's love language?

**Assignment:**

Plan a surprise mini-date for your spouse. Add a personal note about what you love about them.

**Low-Budget Date Ideas:**

- Indoor picnic
- Dance tutorial night
- Dollar store gift exchange

**Group Discussion Application:**

- How has romance changed over the years?
- What are ways to keep it alive without spending money?

Every love story begins with a spark.

# 7

# Intimacy Beyond the Bedroom

**Scripture Focus: 1 Peter 3:7, Proverbs 5:18–19**

Prayer: "Lord, teach us to honor and cherish one another—spirit, soul, and body."

**Reflect & Connect:**

- What makes you feel emotionally safe?

- What helps you feel physically connected to your spouse?

**Assignment:**

Schedule a no-phone evening and just enjoy being together. Talk and laugh with no agenda.

**Low-Budget Date Ideas:**

- Memory lane walk

- Candlelight dessert at home

**Group Discussion Application:**

- What does intimacy look like beyond sex?

- How can couples be more emotionally and spiritually intimate?

*Love bears up under
anything and everything that
comes, is ever ready to believe the
best of every person, its hopes are
fadeless under all circumstances,
and it endures everything
[without weakening].*

**1 Corinthians 13:7**

# 8

# A Prayer Over Your Marriage

**Scripture Focus: Colossians 1:9–14 (AMP)**

Prayer Declaration: (Have couples read this aloud together, alternating lines.)

**Reflect & Connect:**

- What has God shown you about love through this journey?

- What are you praying for your marriage moving forward?

**Assignment:**

Write a Marriage Mission Statement:

"We commit to love, forgive, grow, and serve together by…"

**Group Discussion Application:**

- What's one thing you've learned from another couple in this group?

- What legacy do you want your marriage to leave?

And enduring love
doesn't happen by accident. It's built.
On purpose. With prayer, patience,
forgiveness, fun, and fire.

# Bonus Chapter:

# Continue to Invest In Your Marriage

**Scripture Focus:**

*"For where your treasure is, there will your heart be also."*

—Matthew 6:21 (KJV)

### Let's Talk About It

People naturally take care of what they truly value. Whether it's a home, car, business, or personal health, we spend time and money maintaining what we treasure. The same should be true of our marriage.

When we neglect our marriage, it weakens. But when we invest in it—time, prayer, affection, generosity, communication, and love—it thrives.

No one puts their money into a machine that has an "Out of Order" sign.

If we want our marriage to grow and bring lasting joy, we must bring it into God's divine order. That means building on the foundation of the Word, and aligning with what God says about love, communication, sex, and money.

Order is not bondage. It brings freedom, clarity, peace, and blessing.

# A Word from the Heart

Anything neglected will eventually fall apart. Whether it's a car, a garden, a business—or a marriage—without regular care, things begin to wither. It's the consistent investment that keeps love alive, passion burning, and connection strong.

In Matthew 6:21, Jesus reminds us of a powerful truth: your heart will follow your treasure. That means if you want your heart to stay tender, connected, and in love with your spouse, you must intentionally invest—your time, your words, your resources, your creativity, and your energy.

When you make deposits of love, encouragement, kindness, time, attention, and even finances into your marriage, you're building something of lasting value. Your marriage becomes a well-watered garden—lush, fruitful, and beautiful.

Let this be a gentle reminder that your spouse is worth it. Your marriage is worth it. And God is cheering you on!

# Love Assignment

Take time this week to make a "Love Investment Plan." Together, sit down and choose at least three areas where you can be more intentional about sowing into your marriage. Use the prompts below to help guide your plan.

Here are some categories to consider:

- Time: Schedule undistracted quality time together.

- Words: Speak life-giving, affirming words daily.

- Finances: Plan a simple getaway or save for a special shared goal.

- Prayer: Commit to praying together once a week.

- Learning: Read a marriage book or devotional together.

**My Love Investment Plan:**

1. __________________________________________

   __________________________________________

2. __________________________________________

   __________________________________________

3. __________________________________________

   __________________________________________

## Reflection Questions

Take a few minutes to write honestly and prayerfully:

1. What area of my marriage has received the least attention lately?

❑ Intimacy

❑ Communication

❑ Prayer

❑ Finances

❑ Other: ____________

2. What daily or weekly habit could I begin to help nourish that area?

3. What does investing in our marriage look like for me personally?

4. In what ways can I better honor God's order in our relationship?

## Scripture Study & Discussion

Read and meditate on these verses together:

- Matthew 6:21 – "Where your treasure is…"

- 1 Corinthians 14:40 – "Let all things be done decently and in order."

- Ecclesiastes 4:9-10 – "Two are better than one…"

- Psalm 128:1-4 – "Blessed is everyone who fears the Lord…"

- Colossians 1:9-14 – (Suggested reading aloud together)

## Couples Discussion Prompt:

Which of the scriptures above stood out most to you? Why?

How can we practically apply one of these verses this week in our marriage?

## Scripture Reading Suggestions

• Proverbs 3:5-6 — Trust God in all your ways.

• 1 Corinthians 13 — Love in action.

• Galatians 6:9 — Don't grow weary in doing good.

## Group Discussion: Real Talk

- What are some ways you've seen your marriage thrive when you were consistently investing in it?

- What has been unintentionally neglected in this season?

- How can you support each other better in investing emotionally, spiritually, and practically?

## Group Application:

Create a "Marriage Savings Jar"—a symbolic container where you each write one investment idea per week and drop it in. Share your favorites and commit to doing one each month.

# Interactive Assignment: Your Investment Plan

Together, create a "Marriage Investment Plan" — three simple but intentional ways you will invest in your relationship over the next 30 days.

Our Top 3 Investments This Month:

1. _______________________________________________

_______________________________________________

2. _______________________________________________

_______________________________________________

3. _______________________________________________

_______________________________________________

Pro Tip: Review this list weekly and cheer each other on!

# Low-Budget Date Night Idea

"Memory Lane & Dreams Night" – Grab a cozy blanket, light some candles, and look through old photos or wedding memorabilia. Then dream aloud together: "Where do we want to be in 5 years? What new things would we love to experience together?"

## "DIY Spa Night at Home"

Turn your living room or bedroom into a peaceful mini spa. Light candles, play soft worship or jazz music, and give each other foot rubs or shoulder massages. Finish the night with a sweet treat and a loving prayer together.

## Cut-Out Coupons

Here are a few playful "investment" coupons to cut out and give to your spouse. (Also available as a downloadable printable sheet.)

🕐 "Your Time Is My Treasure" – Redeem for 1 hour of uninterrupted quality time.

💬 "Speak Life" – Redeem for a heartfelt affirmation or love letter.

🎧 "I'm Listening" – Redeem for a distraction-free conversation.

> ✝ "Prayer Partner Pass" – Redeem for a time of prayer together.

> ♥ "Date Night Delight" – Redeem for a homemade date night of your choice.

## Group Application

### Open Group Discussion Questions:

1. What does the word "order" mean to you in marriage?

2. Have you ever felt the effects of neglect in your relationship?

3. What's one testimony you have about how small investments made a big impact in your relationship?

Encourage couples to share testimonies or ideas with each other!

### Closing Reflection & Prayer

*Father God,*

*Thank You for the beautiful gift of marriage. We honor You as the Author of love and the One who brings order to every area of our lives. Today, we recommit ourselves to investing in this covenant You've given us. Show us how to prioritize one another and to treasure our relationship the way You do. Teach us to walk in wisdom and love, to forgive quickly, and to serve joyfully.*

*We ask for fresh grace to walk in Your divine order—freely and joyfully—so that our marriage may flourish and reflect Your goodness.*

*We speak Colossians 1:9–14 over our marriage and our home. Thank You for blessing and strengthening our love.*

*Help us never to take each other for granted. Show us how to keep investing in love with consistency, creativity, and care. Help our hearts stay soft, our words kind, and our actions thoughtful. May our marriage reflect Your goodness and grace.*

In Jesus' name, Amen.

# ♥ *20 Fun & No-Stress Love Coupons for Couples* ♥

*1. Lazy Day Together*
*Redeem for one day of guilt-free rest, snuggles,*
*and no chores.*

*2. You Pick the Movie Night*
*Tonight is all yours—choose the movie, snacks,*
*and cuddle position.*

*3. Love Note Drop*
*Redeem for a handwritten love note tucked*
*somewhere special.*

*4. Breakfast in Bed*
*One homemade breakfast, delivered with*
*love and coffee.*

*5. Uninterrupted Talk Time*
*One hour of distraction-free heart-to-heart conversation.*

*6. Game Night*
*Redeem for a night of your favorite board*
*or card game—winner gets a kiss!*

*7. Dance in the Living Room*
*One slow song (or silly song) and a dance under the lights*
*(or moonlight).*

*8. Evening Walk Together*
*Take a peaceful walk, hand in hand,*
*just the two of you.*

*9. Prayer Together*
*A shared moment of prayer,*
*lifting each other up before God.*

*10. Foot Rub or Back Rub*
*No strings, no rush—just 15 minutes*
*of soothing touch.*

*11. You're Off Duty!*
*Redeem for one night off from dinner,*
*dishes, or the usual task.*

*12. Sweet Treat Run*
*Late-night ice cream? Midnight snack?*
*I've got you covered!*

*13. Compliment Shower*
*Get ready—you're about to receive*
*five genuine compliments.*

*14. You Choose the Music*
*Tonight's playlist is all yours—*
*no veto power!*

*15. DIY Spa Night*
*Face masks, candles, relaxing music—*
*let's pamper each other.*

*16. Memory Lane Moment*
*Let's pull out photos or share our favorite*
*stories from "back then."*

*17. Couch Cuddle & Chill*
*Just us, a cozy blanket, and no phones*
*for one full hour.*

*18. Date Night at Home*
*Set the table, dress up, and act like*
*we're out on the town.*

*19. Surprise Me!*
I'll plan something small and sweet—
just for you.

*20. One Free "I'm Sorry" Pass*
*When grace is needed most—*
*this one's a relationship saver. AA*